Reading Together

Hello, Goodbye

Read it together

This is a gentle, humorous story about making friends. Children will be able to talk about the people they say hello to and the different ways they do this.

Who else do you say hello to?

Hello, Gramps!

I wonder why they are saying goodbye.

They don't want to get wet.

Talking about the book helps children to understand the meanings of the story and the way it is written.

With the repetition of "hello" and "goodbye", children will soon learn to recognize these words and join in the reading.

Hello, hello hello, hello.

As you read, encourage children to use the pictures to work out what will happen next in the story.

The bees said "Hello!" and now...

The bird says "Hello!"

One story can often remind children of other stories they know. See if they'll talk about them and share some of your own.

That bear looks a bit like one of the three bears.

Goldilocks and the three bears.

First published 1988 by Walker Books Ltd
87 Vauxhall Walk, London SE11 5HJ

This edition published 2007

2 4 6 8 10 9 7 5 3 1

Text © 1988 David Lloyd
Illustrations © 1988 Louise Voce
Introductory and concluding notes © 2001 CLPE/LB Southwark

This book has been typeset in Granjon

Printed in China

British Library Cataloguing in Publication Data:
a catalogue record for this book is available
from the British Library

ISBN 978-1-4063-1415-1

www.walkerbooks.co.uk

Hello, Goodbye

Written by
David Lloyd

Illustrated by
Louise Voce

WALKER BOOKS
AND SUBSIDIARIES
LONDON · BOSTON · SYDNEY · AUCKLAND

A tree stood quietly
in the sunshine.

A big brown bear stepped up.
"Hello!" he said, very loudly.

Two bees flew over.
"Hello! Hello!" they said, very busily.

Along came a big red bird.
What did the bird say?
"Hello!" – very quickly.

Soon voices all over
the tree were
saying, "Hello!"

hello

Little voices on the leaves said, "Hello!"

Squeaky voices on the branches said, "Hello!"

Deep-down voices
among the roots
said, "Hello!"

Suddenly a drop of rain
fell on the bear's nose.
Splash!

Raindrops fell all over the bear.
Splash! Splash! Splash!

"Goodbye! Goodbye!"
said the two bees, very busily.
"Goodbye!" said the big red bird,
very quickly.

Goodbye!

goodbye...

goodbye...

goodby

goodbye!

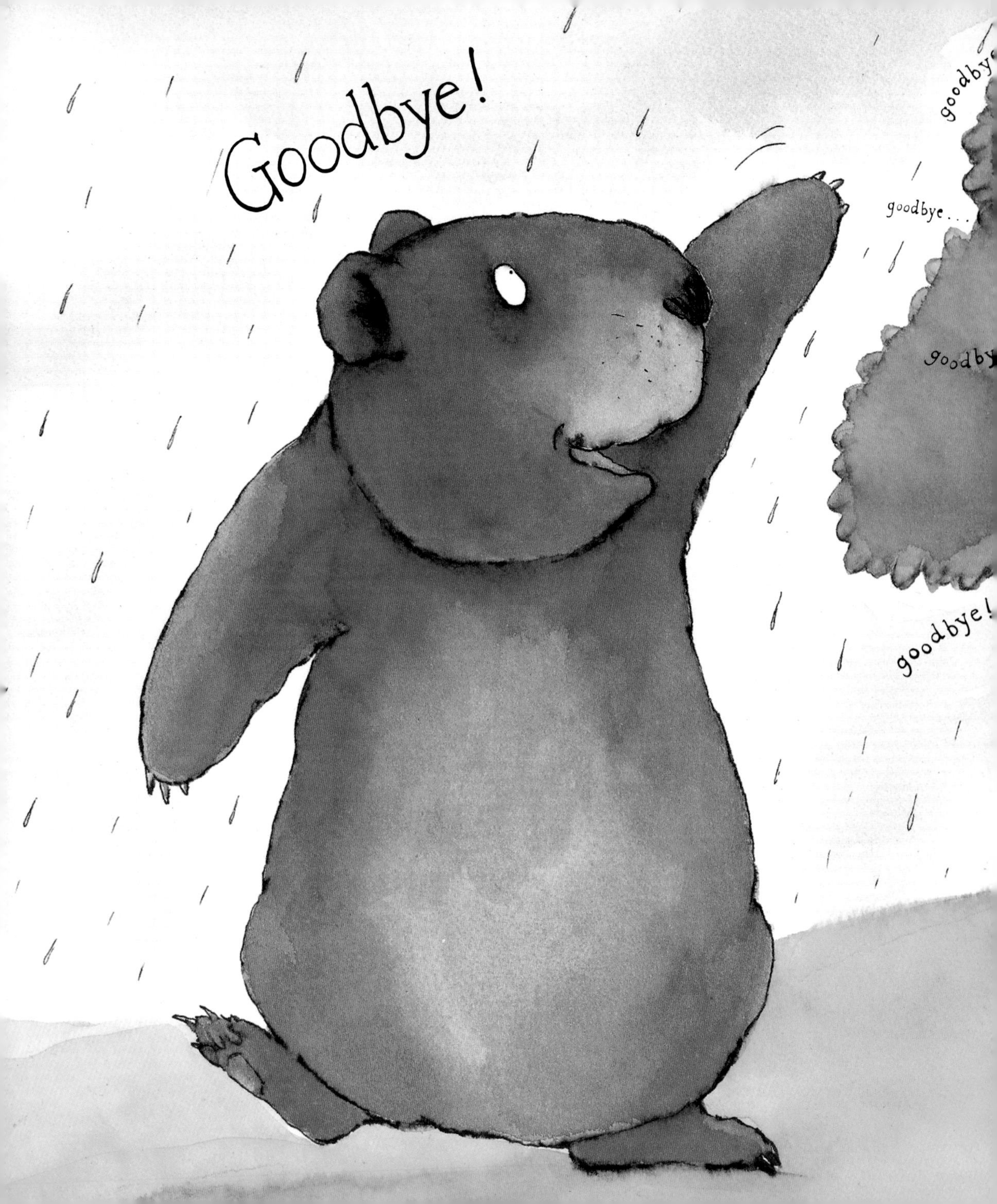

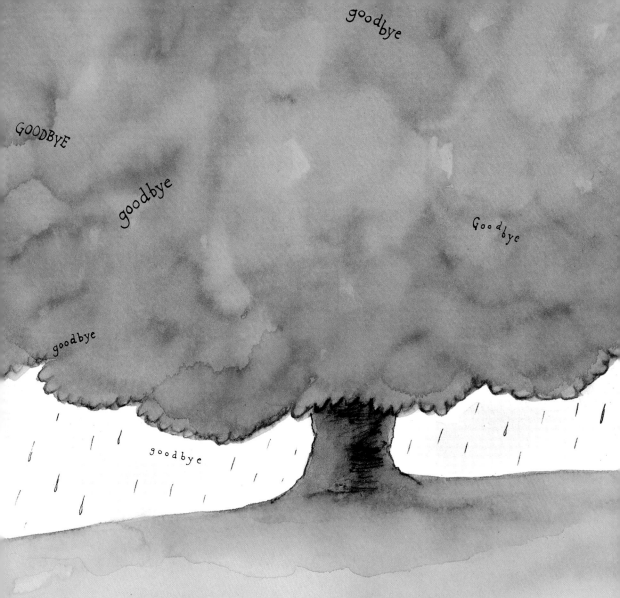

What did all the voices on the tree say?
What did the bear say, very loudly?
"Goodbye!"

Everyone had gone.
The tree stood quietly again.
"Hello, rain!" it said,
very, very quietly.

Read it again

Tell the story
When you've read the book together a few times, you can use the pictures to help your child tell the story in their own words.

What's happening here?

The bees come and say hello to the bear.

What did all the voices on the tree say?

Goodbye, Goodbye, Goodbye...

Taking part
Encourage your child to join in the story by saying "hello" and "goodbye" for each animal. How do you think a squirrel might sound?

"Oh no," said the bear, "it's raining."

Draw a story
With your help, children can paint a picture of the tree. On another piece of paper they can draw the animals and cut them out, then use them to tell this story and make up new ones.

Take a walk

Take a walk in the park and, like the bear, look out for animals. You could make a list together at home. Can you see so many animals when it is raining?

I can see a duck!

Choosing

Encourage your child to talk about the outdoor clothes they need, and which ones are best for sunny or rainy days.

These are for splashing in puddles.

Great, what else do you need?